Tales from the Deep

themes of depth

Featuring:
*John Bartell, Clarissa Cervantes, Daphne Fauber,
Elizabeth Gabel, Janet Guastavino, T. K. Howell,
Ann Howells, A.J. Huffman, Rachel Loughlin,
Ruth Marie-Clair, Claire Massey, Megan Denese Mealor,
David Milley, Sharon Mitchell, James Mulhern,
James B. Nicola, Trish Tyler, Jennifer Weigel,
and Charlotte Young*

All pieces published with permission.
© The Writer's Workout, 2023

Other publications by The Writer's Workout:

Tales from the Cliff
Tales from the Toybox
Tales from the Other Side
72 Hours of Insanity, vols 1-11
Our Pandemic

Quarterly Literary Journal:
WayWords

Look for the next Tales theme in April.

The Writer's Workout is a registered
501(c)(3) nonprofit organization.
We appreciate your support!
www.writersworkout.net

For the

exquisite vastness

of depth.

Table of Contents

Here to the River
    by David Milley 1
Gazing Downward from the Summit
    by Ruth Marie-Clair 3
Remember With the Land
    by Rachel Loughlin 5
Bloop
    by T. K. Howell 7
Outliers
    by Claire Massey 19
The Descent
    by Charlotte Young 21
With Mermaid
    by A.J. Huffman 23
Heeding the Call
    by Ann Howells 25
Brother Fugu
    by Elizabeth Gabel 27
Gravemonger
    by James B. Nicola 31
Of Mermaids and Moonlight
    by A.J. Huffman 33
No More Encores
    by Jennifer Weigel 35
Vilano
    by Megan Denese Mealor 39

Underwater Dreams
>   *by Clarissa Cervantes* 41
Familiar Depths
>   *by Daphne Fauber*..........................43
Last Dive at Wheeler's Branch
>   *by John Bartell*...............................45
The Monster in the Waves
>   *by Janet Guastavino*.......................47
Manual for Mornings
>   *by Sharon Mitchell*.........................49
Piano
>   *by James Mulhern* 51
A Freckle
>   *by Trish Tyler*.................................53

About the Authors...57

About the Editor..65

Here to the River
by David Milley

Muriel speaks: "Life before Ross was easy. Dad doted;
Mother taught me to stand. My mother taught me well.
She told me what the world can be like.
Dad made me kind. Mother made me strong.

Ross was hard at first. He hated the cold.
His mother taught him, too well, what the world can be like.
He swept me from my home. He thought he'd command
my listening smile. I taught him to listen to me.

In his hard way, Ross learned to be kind. All our students,
indeed, all our children, needed us kind. You know
what the world can be like. Together, we lifted them up.

We made hard choices. We knew what the world can be like,
so we went where good people don't go. We lived
with the people the good people shunned. It was cold.
Ross walked with his humbler god, stood with the banished.

Ross is here with me. After he died, I brought his ashes,
alone, here to the river. You know what the world is like.
When our children would visit, we always came here.
Our world flows like the river. Such adventures we lived!

Our children don't return to us now. They brought me here.
We taught them to live their own lives, to be hard and kind.
They lift others. They know what the world can be like."

Gazing Downward from the Summit
by Ruth Marie-Clair

In the calciferous nooks and crevices, the silent
darkness of onus homeostasis, voices of yesterday
bury themselves in the sediment of our ecology.
In the dust of memory, drifting down the purple
mountain of our decadent history, we hear all
all that we have uttered & mumbled & muttered.
From their formless state, our spirits blend the
essence of our ghostly chemistry like concentric
pulses of a star that was never there; the proverbial
tree whose fall we claim to observe but never see.
In the twilight hour, we watch as our quintessence,
like the mists that drool their dew on gossamer, ten-
ors over the lake against the sloshing fugue of its
current and aching sough of its caterwauling depth.
Containers for the sensations of the soul, we stand
apart and figure the speeches hidden in the sacred
sounds of each other's breathing– the hypnotic
dilation of our lungs into and out of their slow acc-
retion– patient as the soft root of a plant that slowly
splits the sidewalk but sacrilegious as the wildflowers
that gather in bristled symmetry when Earth inhales
        to release in exhale over & over & over again.

Remember With the Land
by Rachel Loughlin

The storm laid it bare
The fields planted on mountain soil
Looking so rich, so green
Yet the sudden hard rain devoured
Any place not prepared with
Cover crops and good soil
Deep roots into nourished ground full of life
We watch helplessly
As our efforts wash to the sea

There are no shortcuts
To resiliency
Only hard work and intention and time

And here we are.
The rains are pouring down
Usual resources stripped away
All the places we have been faking flourishing
Tearing off exposing the truth.

Our relationships: shallow
Resources: unsustainable
Schools: inequitable
Cities: divided and unprepared
Our land undernourished

It has forgotten
How to heal itself
It cannot sustain us
No longer remembers
How to save and recreate itself
Over and over again

Futility we try to hold
The earth in place
As it shifts and slips through our hands

Yet, just past fear
On the other side of uncertainty
Something deeper is calling
For turning to a different way

Run the earth between tired fingers
It will whisper what it needs
All this time
It's been trying to teach us
But we were too busy
Now we have time
Close your eyes
Imagine
Remember with the land
How to heal

Bloop
by T. K. Howell

The first thing anyone knew about it was the smell.

Jenkins woke up at four in the morning to check his herd. The scent drifted in on the sea breeze, thick with salt.

The dawn sun speared gold low across the mudflats, hazing in the morning dew. Jenkins put on his wellies and trudged out to the sea wall, his shadow a Colossus stalking behind him. He knew that smell; cloying, sweet, sticking in the back of the throat. At first, he thought he'd lost another heifer in the inlets, stuck and suffocated. But after he'd flushed out his early morning brain with a cup of coffee, he was clear it was something else: the smell was different. Oilier, maybe. A hint of perfume to it.

Jenkins found it just as the sun escaped the bounds of the horizon. He peered over the edge of the seawall and watched as the body was buffeted gently, rhythmically against the concrete by the slowly receding tide.

"Bloody hell," Jenkins muttered to himself.

The ORCA III bobbed in a gentle swell west of Dogger Bank.

"Another one?" Cooper said into the radio receiver.

"Foulness Island, Coop. Same markings. Over." The radio crackled.

"Christ, that's the third one this year," he said in an East Coast rat-a-tat whine. He ruffled his tightly curled grey hair and adjusted his bookish glasses.

"All right. I'll be in as soon as I can. Tell them I want to be involved in the autopsy. Over."

"Coastguard want to blow it up as soon as possible. They're worried the tide'll drift it back into the shipping lanes. Over."

"Christ." Cooper swung the wheel west and headed for the Essex coast.

"Right, which one of you bastards told the Yank?" Dr Carson swung into the office at the Lab wagging her finger. The two interns minimized Twitter and took an intense interest in the reams of data coming in from current meters and underwater microphones dotted around the British coast.

A man in his mid-twenties with a thick, black beard and a nervous disposition shuffled uncomfortably at the other end of the office. "I did it for your own good, Maggie."

"Adil, you little shit."

The two interns snickered. Maggie Carson glared at them.

"Come on, at your time of life you've got to be grasping these opportunities with both hands," Adil pleaded.

"My time of life? *My time of life?* Young man, I'd appreciate it if you didn't concern yourself with my private life and whatever my hands choose to grasp, which right now might be your throat. We better beat him there or he'll compromise the carcass, the man has a terrible disregard for scientific process. Get the Land Rover. Just for that, you're driving. Chrissie, Jonas, I want all the data for the last week on shipping, oil drilling, and any seismic activity in the North

Sea. Send it to my PDA as soon as you have it. Adil, bring your waders, your shoulder-length gloves, and a chainsaw. You're going to get a bit messy."

Adil gathered up his stuff and glumly headed for the car park.

Farmer Jenkins was making a tidy sum by the evening, charging people five pounds to take the route across his land to the sea wall. It was all over Twitter by the time the Land Rover rolled into the farm.

"'Who are you lot?" he asked.

"We're with the British Oceanographic Data Centre," Adil said, leaning out of the window. "Aren't you expecting us?"

"Then who's the t'other bugger down there up to his elbows in the bloody thing?"

"Cooper. Bloody Cooper's beat us here," Maggie said. In the background, they heard the whine of a chainsaw kicking into life.

The Land Rover pulled up. There was a crowd of about thirty leaning over the wall, clad in cagoules and windbreakers, braced against the drizzle drifting in off the North Sea. Maggie Carson strode out to yell down at Matt Cooper.

"What the bloody hell do you think you're doing? You don't have any authority to be here!"

Cooper cupped his hand to his ear defenders as the chainsaw idled. He squinted and shrugged his shoulders.

"Turn the bloody thing off!"

I can't hear you, Cooper mouthed. His feet were sloshing in a few inches of water and his once-white whole-body protective suit was splattered with grey and red streaks. Underneath the helmet, and through the visor, the only thing visible was his circle-rimmed glasses and the grey stubble around his broad smile.

"You lot, out of my way. I'm a scientist!" Maggie pushed her way to a small steel ladder and climbed ungainly down to the beach below.

"Maggie, are you sure you should be-"

"Adil, so help me God if you use the phrase '*at your time of life'* ever again, I'm having you shipped out to the Arctic research department."

Maggie strode towards the huge, bloated body wagging her finger at the man brandishing a chainsaw. Cooper sheepishly turned off the engine, took off his helmet, and pulled back the hood on his outfit.

"Margot! Glad you could make it."

"Don't call me that Coop, you shit. You know I could have you arrested for this? Do you even have a license for operating that chainsaw?"

Cooper laughed a nerdish little laugh that brought his shoulders up somewhere around his ears. Maggie glared at him.

"Oh don't look at me like that," Cooper said. "You know I'll melt. Now then, would you like me to tell you what we've got? Young adult female Sperm Whale-"

"Yes, I can see that, thank you very much."

"Approximately twenty-six feet in length. Dead probably forty-eight hours or so, given the level of bloating. Ostensibly healthy. Stomach contents-" Cooper gestured at the gloopy mass by his feet, "Squid. A lot of squid. Cause of death: I don't know about you, but I'm going to hazard a guess it's these three gashes leading from the anterior of the head to the base of the jaw, which has been almost completely severed. What caused that I hear you ask? Well, how's about we ask the gallery? Geoff up here-" Cooper pointed to an overweight man with a thick red beard leaning over the wall, "-has a theory. What was it, Geoff?" Cooper shouted up to the wall.

"Megalodon."

"Ah, but Geoff, I'm afraid I'm going to have to disagree with you there." Cooper wagged a finger at the man. "The wounds, you see," Cooper gestured at the Sperm whale's head, "are not in the familiar circular pattern of a shark bite. Besides, as you well know, Megalodon is extinct. You've been spending too much time on YouTube. How about you there, Jason was it?" Cooper waved up at a skinny, pale teen with reddened eyes.

"Cthulhu," he said. He looked like he was trying not to be sick.

"Ha ha.."

"Have you quite finished showing off?" Maggie interrupted, folding her arms.

"I haven't even got to the Canvey Island Monster yet," Cooper grinned.

"Well it's not one of your bloody sharks, that's for sure." Maggie took a huge gulp of Stout. There was only one small pub in the area and the three of them had decamped there for the evening. In the morning, the Coastguard would tow the body out to deeper water, cram it with dynamite and blow it to pieces.

"On London's doorstep. Press will be all over this. You know what they get like."

Adil nursed a diet coke. Cooper, after a long scrub had managed to get the bits of whale out of his hair and was on his third bottle of weak lager. Maggie had rolled her eyes.

"Not a shark." Maggie wiped the foam from her top lip. "Adil here's a fan of yours, Coop."

"I'm glad someone is."

"Read all your books. That silly yachting thing you won and that crap you pulled off Martha's Vineyard. Even listens to the *podcasts.*"

There was a nasty, mocking tone to Maggie's voice. Adil suddenly felt the need to be somewhere else. "I'll… erm… I'll get a round in."

Alone, Maggie and Coop tried not to meet each other's eyes.

"Uh-"

"What?"

"Err… em. Nothing. Nothing."

"Oh don't sulk," Maggie snapped. "What did you expect, that I'd just wait around for you while you spent half of every year at sea?"

"Didn't say a thing," Cooper answered.

"You smell of rotting whale blubber. Don't even think about-"

"Didn't say a thing," Cooper repeated.

"And all this crap you're doing now? You used to be a serious researcher once. And look at you now! This sea monster stuff is embarrassing. And the TokTiking, the social media stuff? Act your age."

"Maybe, but my book sales have gone up by around eight hundred percent in the last two years."

Maggie shook her head in disappointment. On the table, her PDA flashed a message. She turned away from

Cooper and scrolled through the tables of data the interns had sent through.

"Urgh."

"What?"

"It's just... I know how you're going to react. Look here," Maggie turned the screen around. "Picked up by underwater microphone arrays in Tyne, Viking, Forties, and a station on the Fair Isles about three days ago. A repeating low-frequency sound starting around six hertz and rising to thirty. That's travelled at least a thousand miles from the source? Possibly further? That's-"

"At the very limit of Blue Whale vocalisation," Adil interrupted setting down the drinks.

"Where?" Cooper asked.

"Chrissie says here she's triangulated it to about two hundred miles off the coast of Norfolk. And *here* and *here*, look, just before the last two whales washed up."

"Bloop!" Cooper yelped.

"What?" Maggie said, deadpan.

"Bloop! Yes, yes, yes," Cooper banged the table excitedly. "Hang on, I know I've got files on this somewhere. Yes, here we go," he said, fishing a tablet out of his bag. "Ever since we started recording the ocean, ever since we started listening to whale songs, there have been anomalous calls. Outliers. Calls that are louder and lower than anything we have been able to attribute to known species. It has been postulated that these are the calls of some deep-sea species of Cetacean. Possibly a prehistoric remnant."

"Knew it," Maggie grunted. "Why are you doing this? Why have you started believing all this... this... *crap*. What happened to you?"

"Oh no, I didn't say I believed any of it." Cooper waved his hands animatedly. "But it's an interesting theory, isn't it? You know what they say about the bottom of the world's oceans and the dark side of the moon and all that."

"The lunatics are in my hall."

"Har dee har," Cooper curled his lip.

"I don't get it," Adil said.

"Too young, kiddo! Too young. Look, I'm not saying there's a Basilosaur on the loose in the North Sea or anything like that, but we're scientists, right?"

"Some of us still are, at least."

Cooper ignored Maggie. "We theorise, we investigate, we evaluate. In 1986 a Soviet Sub-"

"Oh god, here we go. Strap yourself in Adil, it's story time with Cooper. Don't get him started or he'll show you his scars."

"Thank *you,* Margot. In 1986, K-219, a Soviet Sub, picked up strange noises – Quakers, they called them – and was then struck by a mystery object in open deep water. They wrote it up as a clash with a US sub, but there were none in the area. K-219 went down as they evacuated with sixteen nuclear warheads. When they sent a Deep-Sea exploration vehicle down to investigate, they found three huge gashes down the Port side."

"Woah," Adil gawped.

"Oh behave, Coop. So what, you think a 'Bloop' or a 'Quacker' killed our Sperm Whale?"

"I don't know. I... I think it's time for me to turn in. I'll see you in the morning by the carcass, right?"

"You always were an old romantic."

Maggie woke at six on the dot without a hangover. It was six-thirty by the time she'd showered and had a coffee. By the time she'd managed to bang on Adil's door, wake him up and get him down to the sea wall it was already eight.

"It's gone."

"I can see that."

"Tide?"

"Coastguard."

"They were supposed to give us until noon!"

"Adil, you are a lazy so and so. I suppose you didn't have time to check the morning news? I suppose you were too tired on the drive over to notice the three rather lost-looking vans with transmitters sticking out all over the place? I suggest you have a look at that Twitter thing of yours."

Adil dug out his phone. "#foulnessbeast. Bloody 'ell. Oh hells, Maggie. Oh hells, this shit has blown up!"

"Not quite yet." Maggie pointed back west toward the city. "Listen." On the breeze, there was the *whumph-whumph* of a helicopter approaching.

Minutes later it roared overhead and raised out over the sea without stopping. Adil squinted.

"There!"

A moment later there was a soft *Crumph* noise. They could just make out the jet of water spear into the sky as the helicopter circled for a better shot.

"Adil."

"Yes, Doctor Carson?"

"Where the hell is Coop?"

"Aboard the ORCA III, I'd guess."

"And where would you guess the ORCA III is right now?"

"Probably about two hundred miles off the Norfolk coast."

World Famous Oceanographer Among Missing in Hunt for Mystery Beast.

Adil had been hiding the paper all day, but he couldn't screen her calls. Interview requests came in every half hour, emails every five minutes. The first reporter tried to doorstop him at the lab two days after the whale was left strewn over the Foulness coast.

"Stupid bugger," was all Maggie would say about Cooper.

A storm had kicked up the afternoon Cooper set out and there had been no contact from the ORCA III, or two other privately chartered ships that had somehow got wind of the initial triangulation. So far, no wreckage had been found.

The Director of the BODC called Adil when he couldn't get a hold of Maggie. The interest had reached a fever pitch. #foulnessbeast was still trending.

"It's a bloody circus. What is it, silly season? Is it a slow news week or something? I didn't think we had them anymore. This monster business is making us a laughing stock the longer we stay quiet about it. I've set up a small press conference for Dr Carson-"

"I'm not sure Mag- I mean, Dr Carson, is in a position to-"

"Well bloody well get her in position, son. Unless you want posting to the Arctic station."

Adil sighed. He didn't know why everyone seemed so keen on sending him to the Arctic.

They sent down the big PR guns from the Head Office to shepherd Maggie through the process. They handed her the Director's carefully scripted statement and guided her into the small conference room. There were a handful of carefully selected reporters seated, not the wild gaggle of flashing cameras and clicking dictaphones bad TV crime dramas had led her to expect.

"It is the finding of the British Oceanographic Data Centre that there is no conclusive evidence of a-" Maggie sighed audibly, "*sea monster.* The recent whale beachings on the East Coast are more than likely the result of-"

"Hang on, but what about the sound recordings?"

"No interruptions, please. We will take questions at the end," one of the PR guns snapped.

"And the claw marks?"

"What about Matt Cooper, an experienced sailor, vanishing in the exact spot that-"

"With the loss of an American citizen, there has been a Tweet from-"

"Oh shut up." Maggie stood up abruptly, pushing her chair back. "Enough of this utter crap. It'd be easier, wouldn't it? Easier to believe there's something out there doing this. Easier to believe in the crackpot theories about the Canvey Island Monster, or Bloop or whatever they're calling it. Otherwise, it's just chaos."

"What Dr Carson means to say-" the PR gun began, but Maggie cut her off with a wave of her hand.

"I know bloody well what I mean to say, thank you. That's where this all spouts from, a need for an answer, a simple—albeit mysterious—answer to the difficult questions. Well, I'm afraid there is a simple answer; Cooper was lost in a storm, the Foulness whale and the two before it were hit by

17

propellers because they strayed into a shipping lane when naval testing in the North Sea disorientated them. Turns out our intern did her sums wrong. In fact, the 'Bloop' was an iceberg calving in Greenland. Another one. Because of climate change. Those are the answers. Those are what the data is telling us. But you want a monster, don't you? You want something to blame? Well go home and take a long hard look in the mirror."

      Maggie tucked her folder under her arm and calmly walked out of the press conference.

Outliers
by Claire Massey

Snorkeling past the divemaster's whistle,
Trinidad fades
to outline shaded
where jungle erupts,
no hint of interiors lush with scarlet ibis,
poinciana forest.

I float in the original womb
over gardens of staghorn coral blooming
with rainbow wrasse and fairy basslet,
intruder in a queendom ruled
by angelfish and barracuda.

The iguanas whose place it is
to recycle seeds of papaya,
the frigate birds who rule the air
above Mayaro, leafcutter ants
who work their metropolis unaware
of diners on verandahs overhead,
blind moles who tunnel under
golden shower trees
do not know this liquid warmth,
the buoyancy of salt.

Before me yawns a chasm shaded

cerulean-blue to black,
a launching slip atop a cliff
of continental shelf.

I move my hands in figure 8s,
quiet pumping legs.
Purple fans that guard the brink
wave me ahead
but I feel colder borders, understand,
I'm ill equipped to venture past them.

I turn back for the boat,
the captain's count of souls,
the dry towel and box lunch.

Shore bound with all aboard,
the first mate tells us stories.
I take on faith his word
that bioluminescent creatures roam
sunless depths below
and ichthyologists discovered
opahs, warm-blooded fish,
flapping heated fins like wings,
swimming unmapped leagues beyond
the boundaries of their niche.

The Descent
by Charlotte Young

The suit makes me less man than machine
But I don the helmet like a somber crown.
I secure my line to the submarine
And I descend, down down down.

The water is chilling and abysmal.
Nothing good could exist here.
I can feel the infinite silence chisel
At my mind until I only fear fear fear.

Deep down I know I should return.
Why did I descend into this icy grave?
I summon my courage and spurn
Myself on to be brave brave brave

I continue my journey, and a voice
Calls me away from retreat.
My new friend gives me a choice,
To freeze in life or to sleep sleep sleep.

The water is no longer thin and cold,
It is a warm embrace I cannot resist.
The smiling one is something to behold,
My thoughts are fading into mist mist mist.

I cannot find he who found me,
But I will let myself drift under his sight.
He would never hurt me so I will not flee,
Even as his arms wrap so tight tight tight.

I've never felt so loved and held so dear.
He snaps my line. My heart fills with dread.
I turn on my light and inspect my gear.
The water is not black but red red red.

The quiet whisper in my mind now screams,
An unholy wail that suffocates my will.
His smiling face still beams,
Now he only wants to kill kill kill.

I twist and squirm to try and go back
But he begins to slowly squeeze.
I feel my ribs buckle and crack
And now I can't breathe breathe breathe.

A diver who dove too close to the devil,
A sailor whose soul he prayed to keep.
All victims of the ancient vessel.
All souls lost to the deep deep deep.

With Mermaid
by A.J. Huffman

mindset, I sacrifice myself
to the sea, open my arms to embrace
salted consumption of waves welcoming
me to battle. Rocks help me
to shed this skin for another,
shinier shell. I can finally breathe
here in the aquatic depths. In should-be
death, I am finally finding home.

Heeding the Call
by Ann Howells

Tidal pools drained, sang melodies
atonal and aleatoric
haunting echoes filled her head.
How long she curled into herself
as tides rose and ebbed.
Sun could not warm her
and moon's myriad reflections
paved a path across the waves.
She trembles in shadows of sharks
whirls the sandy floor
hair writhing among starfish
urchins, and scallop shells
gliding past life, past memory
past ferryboats and pleasure craft
at rest beneath salty water—
snug wooden coffins.

Watermen murmur
their unintelligible dialect,
catch hands in massed hair, lift her,
lashes aglitter, moon-glazed eyes staring.
A sister wails, will never understand
that now her spirit leaps, unfettered
sailfish above unfurled wave
glistening like an opal.

Brother Fugu
by Elizabeth Gabel

The water was dark and murky when I met Brother Fugu. I think that is why he came, even though I couldn't see him at first. He was built not to be seen, so it really wasn't my fault. His head was square with puffy white lips and big round eyes that never blinked. His skin was mottled gray with uniform black spots. Once I saw him I never missed him again.

At first I didn't know why he came to me, but he swam calmly ahead, his gossamer fins beating so fast they were more of a blur than an object I could define with lines and colors. He stayed ahead of me, but would turn and look at me with his unblinking eyes to make sure I was still there– following. I was.

Occasionally, he would hover over a spot giving me time to discover the life around us; tiny blue and silver fish in schools like rain, or long thick green eels that were the stuff of nightmares. The coral reflected the sunlight giving it a glow. He was proud of his metropolis, the golden reef, and wanted to show it off. I obliged and soon I was there every day, waiting for my tour and he would tell his stories.

Some days the water was agitated by the rains from the above world and I could not see much, but sometimes, especially in the early afternoons when that warm yellow light filtered down to his reef, it was spectacular. Our little tours, or not so much tours anymore, but rather meanderings, were long and so slow some would think we weren't moving at all.

I was proud too, of my elegant white fins and my slow rhythmic breathing that moved with the gentle sway of the ocean's heartbeat. I lied to myself that I had always belonged there, healing in the shallows of the deep blue. But I didn't.

As time passed, Brother Fugu came and went, sometimes leading others on their tours. I was jealous, but had learned enough to make my own way, peaking in corners and crevices to find life. My world soon dissolved away into his.

Time slowed and eventually stopped. There was only the reef and only the gentle sound of my heart beat. Brother Fugu came to me and we settled into the cadence of the sea's song making our way over the familiar terrain.

He turned to me, eyeing me carefully, and gently, almost imperceptibly, changed course. At first I didn't notice, but it didn't too take long as the reef took on a different look. It was a path we had never taken. Curious, but accepting, I followed. No reason to question him.

The reef thinned until it was no more. Eventually, the sandy bottom, home to sharp-teethed barracuda, gave way to a lifeless rocky flat. Still, I did not question his choices, looking forward to new adventure. Deeper and deeper we went, where the yellow sun was barely discernible. There was no current, no rhythmic beating of the sea's heart just silence and growing dark.

The flat gave way to a steep drop, to a canyon larger than any in the above world. For the first time I hesitated, confused. This was a part of the deep blue I had no desire to visit, for the dark was deep, sucking the light from all the corners. I could not see beyond a few short feet. I looked at him with questions he did not answer. He turned and stared with his large round eyes, beckoning me with only a glint. Hesitantly, I followed.

Although I knew I could not fall, I felt untethered as I languidly slipped down, passing layered maps of life in the walls. Iridescent creatures with bulging eyes, or no eyes at all, did their day's work, ignoring me. It was a mystery: the strange animals, the dark, and most of all, the quiet. It was ultimate peace, and from that the ultimate rest.

I do not know if they found my body in the above world. It doesn't matter.

Gravemonger
by James B. Nicola

The creatures of the sea must understand
it as a spring of life and death at once
by strategies to hide beneath the sand,
change colors or direction, or squirt ink,
or the instinctive flinches of a school.

I lie beside the sea, hear, feel a pulse
hypnotic in its restorative hymn,
the peace betrayed by grisly knowledge as
my feet get tickled. The salt water stretches
as fingers reaching from a grave. They'd pull
me in at first then, like sea monsters, climb

up, swallowing my toes, then ankles, inch
by inch, seducing. But wet plashes wake
me back to an awareness. Whew. I'm safe:
the almanac says a neap tide is due.
At first I brace the ministrations like
massage, then clamber up to higher land.

I like to lie beside a sea and fool
myself that all I need's to feel, not think—
to lie, but not be lulled into a trance
so thick that I would not be roused from sleep
in time, but be devoured by the deep.

originally published in
Among the Satyrs and Nymphs
(Bibliotheca Alexandrina, 2020)

Of Mermaids and Moonlight
by A.J. Huffman

Midnight in the middle of the ocean is an exercise
in monotony. Minds wander to magical tales,
legends of ladies wearing nothing but scales. Clocks
tick like hammers, forcing tired eyes to remain
open, on watch for possible disaster. Clouds open
and close, doorways to other worlds. Winds whisper
into ears drowning in redundancy of waves. The words
sound like a woman's song, ring like a reflection
of something silver in the water. Following
its call one step too far means death. The depth
of possibility is too much for most men to ignore.

No More Encores
by Jennifer Weigel

Dear Poseidon,

    I am writing this as a formality more than anything. I shall try to remain professional, and I shall try not to let my emotions sway my ability to write this letter of resignation in a composed manner.
    As you already know, I am quitting. This letter marks my official notice. I am resigning from my post and finally taking my leave. I am unwilling to continue to play "clean up crew" or to do your dirty work.
    When I took this position with my sisters, we had a clear directive. We were eager to engage in the world of men and to have a purpose. Let me remind you of the job description.

    Lure men to their deaths in a watery grave by singing sweetly to the sailors to lull them to sleep. Descend upon them as they lay on their ships, tear them to pieces, and feast upon their flesh.

    My sisters and I thought this would be the perfect opportunity to put our talents to use. We had long wished to find an outlet for our music and to captivate audiences with our stage presence and songwriting skills. And we hungered for flesh to fill our untoward desires.

This was the best partnership we could imagine; part Classical, part Rock 'n' Roll, part Punk, all hedonistic partying... Zeus, Hades and you yourself all throw quite the shindigs, and to have opportunity to play a part in that, well... We couldn't wait to start.

It's hard for a girl band to get a break, let alone a girl band of monstrous beasts, especially starting out. It seems you have to bear your breasts to every talent agent, director, or exec you cross paths with. This outlet was a perfect fit. The representation was great. The record label was top notch. We had to sign.

And for centuries, this was a great gig. But times have changed.

The world of mankind is drastically different. My home, my ocean, is not at all what it once was. This change is not the result of my actions luring men to their deaths. Quite the contrary! They don't need our coaxing to ensure their own demise at sea. They embark on the open ocean in makeshift dinghies that don't need any help to capsize, set their own refugee rafts aflame, and leave their comrades adrift to drown at sea.

Flotsam and jetsam litter my shoreline. Men are constantly dumping the stuff, whether they intend to or not. There is an island of garbage in the Pacific Ocean larger than my home base. My fellow sea creatures perish from eating tiny bits of detritus.

And I won't go into the oil tankers. I refuse to bear witness to another oil tanker or rig disaster. Especially not after what happened to my sisters.

But I digress. This is not the job we took when we signed on with you. To reiterate, we weren't hired on as clean up crew. We didn't expect to be wrangling bits of barbed metal hooks and fishing line out of the fins of sea turtles, rescuing entangled seals, or prying plastic ring connectors from around the throats of seabirds.

The groupies have left. The stagehands are gone. My sisters are dead. I am tired of playing housemaid. I have amassed enough vacation that this two-week notice marks the start of my holiday before I retire to the Styx. Upon receipt of this letter, I am gone.

Send in the Kraken. Let Davy Jones do your dirty work. As for The Sirens, we are through.

For Eternity,
Thelxiepeia

Vilano

by Megan Denese Mealor

On the beach that night,
the wind crawling in shudders
between the dunes,
we sank into the crevices
of a raven's eye moon
bleeding sonnets on the sand.
We made hasty love in the shallow tide,
the saltwater stinging,
cleaning you out of me,
rushing you into me.

Sometimes, when the ocean freezes,
stunned into undulation,
it remembers our heartbeats,
deeper than a leatherback diving,
with more electricity
than a Bluefire jellyfish
defending the sea.

Underwater Dreams
by Clarissa Cervantes

Glimpses of you
in my underwater dreams
where everything moves
a bit slower,
it seems…
The silence breaks
as I reach the surface
for a breath of fresh air
just to go deep again
into our ocean of love…
Not shallow love
we like the depths of strong currents,
tossing and turning into our future…
we have found each other
among so many others,
Creatures whispering…
Currents twisting…
She finally swam close
the rest was history,
just like her
he too had fins.

Familiar Depths
by Daphne Fauber

Don't you know? Your smile is an undertow
serene on the surface, hiding my demise.
Yet I freedive in—danger worth the prize—
gripping a burden to carry me below,
soon made breathless but afraid to let go,
sink deeper and deeper into your grotto.
Despite your deceit, imagine my surprise
when my chest is choked with your drawn-out deathblow.

"This time I'm prepared," I promise as I dive,
bearing a deep sea suit and a lengthy line,
dropping my burden, confident to arrive,
devoutly pay respects to your secret shrine.
The disloyal current on my cord entwines
leaving me suffocated in your divine.

Last Dive at Wheeler's Branch
by John Bartell

On the third pass
you pet the cement back
of the armadillo,
a marker that someone had dropped
into this hill country lake,
minnows nipping on the algae
that has made a home
on this foreign object,
bubbles rising from your tank
as you laugh and twirl
like a ten-year-old girl on a swing.

It's hard to believe,
sitting here now,
with you, in the sun, sipping this beer,
but they say the lake froze clear across,
earlier this year,
when cold came
and the pipes burst all around us
like fireworks
in the summer sky.

I would have liked to have been there,
in the snow,
the stillness of it all

hiding the truth,
that under the sheen of ice,
lie a cement statue,
one you would pat
to let me know
how lost
I was.

The Monster in the Waves
by Janet Guastavino

Each day I surf a wave of terror, cresting by a world that is relentless in its ravenous humor. I try to be mindful in the moment but each moment is horrifying. More often than not, I squeeze my eyes shut and hope what is advancing isn't real. Alas, it *always* is and soon I am yet again wounded by its ferocity. This monster is the creature I fear the most, over which I have no control, and that brings me to my knees in the scow carrying me from birth to death and beyond. As that is the span of time we inhabit, perhaps there is a time beyond consciousness in which I was not, am not, will not be pursued and pulled under by a force greater than my ability to tread water. I drown, I drown.
I am falling into the darkness of the deep.

Manual for Mornings
by Sharon Mitchell

In the morning,
I like to rise slowly.
Slowly, I said.

So if you are up before me,
don't come at me
with your questions,
your to-do list, your pawing,
or what you heard on the news,

when I'm not ready,
when my consciousness
is still creaking its way
up from the ocean floor,
a deep-sea submersible
on a rusty old cable
trailing seaweed
and tiny silvery fish.

That is where I go
when I'm asleep—
into the deep dark,
the comforting silence
of the abyss.

The return must take place
in its own time, or else
my brain gets the bends.
I will snarl like a sea lion.
and I will not be sorry,
because I told you.

But I want to know
you're there, my ship
waiting for me on the surface.
Touch me as you walk by.
Sit beside me on the bed
while you put on your shoes.
Lie down with me
one last time, so I can reach
for your hull as I wake.

Piano
by James Mulhern

On that gray day, you chopped the Steinway piano with an ax.
Surrounded by yellow and red leaves on the hard earth,
you raised your arm to smash it all apart.

I could only wonder. You were a man raised to think
crying was weak. Strength and power should define you.
Men like you couldn't voice their secrets or despair.

You shattered the instrument, exorcising its shiny veneer.
Resin-impregnated paper, dovetail joints, wooden ribs,
and polished mahogany scattered around you.

Slowly the curved outline of the piano became a ragged mess.
The soundboard heart cracked. Small planks of air-dried wood
joined the miscellany of strings, keys, and padded hammers.

I thought of my mother, the day she moved out,
how you changed the locks and emptied every closet,
destroying each vestige of your shared lives.

If I had left the window to join you outside,
I would have seen your tears,
glistening strings on the soundboard of a broken soul.

A Freckle
by Trish Tyler

I stare and look at myself in the mirror. I see it peeking out from underneath my bra. A freckle. However, it's not just any freckle. It is black. It is deep. It is a permanent. It is sobering.

A freckle, always a pale apple red, lays upon my skin. Proudly, it stands out from my pink sun-kissed chest. This freckle though is different. It's not a badge of a vibrant, healthy youth. It's as dark as my future now seems.

It's a tattoo. Not the cool, fun type of a regretful teenage romance. It's a symbol, a marker. It was against my will. It wasn't something I wanted or asked for. Yet here I am. With this tattoo, as well as 6 of its sisters.

This tattoo assists the technician focusing the radiation to my breast. This tattoo helps the technician to not accidentally miss and "hit my heart", causing heart ailments as I age. What's the worst that could happen? I already have cancer. Besides, that heart disintegrated a long time ago with the diagnosis.

"Things can be worse", I was told. "At least, you won't lose your hair. Oh, by the way. Is there any way you can move your surgery to a different day? After all, it's Christmas. Aren't you afraid, you'll ruin Christmas."

"Can you reschedule your appointments until after work?" My boss drones at me. Each dose of radiation to that freckle cooks me from the inside out. Each dose exhausts me in a way I have never felt before. Each dose makes me cry. I know that I never miss a day of work. I also know deep in my heart; my job before my obituary hit social media.

Each dose to that freckle is another thousand dollars I go deeper in debt. It's another reminder that I had "the good cancer" and that I "look like I've always been healthy". Yet, every morning I now wake up with arthritic fervor. When will I feel better? Will I ever feel better. I want to die.

I am not allowed to wallow, to grieve a future that now seems out of focus and dim. I have to pull it together. I am needed by my son, my husband, my widowed father. I must be strong for them. If I am weak, I am out of luck.

I don't know how I feel anymore. This freckle is definitive. It represents a world, a future that doesn't seem so open and expansive.

The freckle represents my hatred of pink. I never liked it. I still don't. It's my hatred of the words "warrior" and "brave". Those words preclude that I chose this fight.

This freckle represents a morning seen differently. The sun rises differently. The light creeps through the bedroom window and illuminates my son's face. I've made it another day. I am alive to see another day.

"It will be fine," they say. The doctors assure me. They must think I am the most childish, selfish, vain person in the world. "No one will notice," they say. They promise after all, it just looks like a freckle.

About the Authors

John Bartell

John Bartell is an east coast transplant trying to make it Texas, drinking Shiner beer and enjoying the Austin music scene, though he hasn't taken to wearing cowboy boots. You can find his poetry in journals such as *The Orchards Poetry Review*, *Canyon Voices*, *The Loch Raven Review*, *Rat's Ass Review*, *Blue Hole Poetry Anthology* and *Muddy River Poetry Review*.

Clarissa Cervantes

Clarissa Cervantes is a poet, photographer, physical therapist and researcher. Clarissa strives to create meaningful articles to inspire and uplift readers. Clarissa holds a B.A. in Physical Therapy, where she found her vocation to help as well as to deliver comfort to people through her images and words. For Clarissa, every poem written is an open invitation to readers to look closely, question more and find beauty and gratitude in their daily lives.

Daphne Fauber

Daphne Fauber (she/her) is a queer writer, artist, and microbiologist based out of Indiana. Her work has been published in the *Garfield Lake Review*, *The Last Girls Club* Magazine, *Permafrost* Magazine, and *Diet Milk* Magazine.

She can be found on Instagram at @daphne.writes, Chill Subs at Daphne Fauber, or at her website www.dank.pizza.

Elizabeth Gabel
    Author declined a bio.

Janet Guastavino
    Janet Guastavino is a fifth-generation San Franciscan and a graduate of UC Berkeley, where she researched and earned a degree in Women's and Ethnic Studies. Along the way, she has raised two children, performed in a Celtic music band, and learned a lot about limitations and possibilities. She has been writing poetry for the past fifteen years and has been published digitally and in hard copy.

T. K. Howell
    T. K. Howell lives on the banks of the Thames and manages ancient oak woodlands, tending to trees that are older than most countries. His writing is often inspired by mythology and folklore and can be found at various genre and literary spaces including *Lucent Dreaming, Mystery* Magazine, *Firewords* and *Indie Bites*.

Ann Howells
    Ann Howells edited *Illya's Honey* for eighteen years. Recent books are: *So Long As We Speak Their Names* (Kelsay Books, 2019) and *Painting the Pinwheel Sky* (Assure Press, 2020). Chapbooks include: *Black Crow in Flight*,

Editor's Choice in *Main Street Rag*'s 2007 competition and *Softly Beating Wings*, 2017 William D. Barney Chapbook Competition winner (Blackbead Books). Her work appears in small press and university publications including *Plainsongs, Schuylkill Valley Journal,* and *San Pedro River Review*. Ann is an eight time Pushcart nominee.

A.J. Huffman
    Author declined a bio.

Rachel Loughlin
    Rachel Loughlin graduated from Virginia Commonwealth University where she received the Undergraduate Poetry Award. She is a graphic designer, eternally optimistic gardener, runner, muralist, and writer living in Richmond, Virginia. Rachel explores the intersections of nature, sensuality, and deconstructed spirituality through her poetry. Her work appears in *Pure Slush Books, Green Ink Poetry, Tiny Seed Literary Journal, Paddler Press, Michigan State Library, Moss Piglet, Fathom, Plum Tree Tavern, Kind of a Hurricane Press,* and others.

Ruth Marie-Clair
    Author declined a bio.

Claire Massey
    Claire Massey's poetry, flash fiction, and short memoir have appeared in over thirty journals of the visual and literary

arts. She is passionate about eco-poetry that inspires environmental activism. Previously a selection editor for *The Emerald Coast Review,* she is currently poetry editor for *The Pen Woman* magazine.

Megan Denese Mealor
Megan Denese Mealor echoes and erases in Jacksonville, Florida. A three-time Pushcart Prize nominee and current Best of the Net candidate, her writing has been published in literary journals worldwide, most recently *The Decadent Review, Moot Point Magazine, Book of Matches,* and *The Wise Owl.* Megan has also authored three poetry collections: *Bipolar Lexicon* (Unsolicited Press, 2018); *Blatherskite* (Clare Songbirds Publishing House, 2019); and *A Mourning Dove's Wishbone* (Cyberwit, 2022). She is currently reading submissions for *Autumn House Press, Uncharted, Pencilhouse, Suburbia Journal,* and *The Common.* Megan lives with her husband Tony, their 9-year-old son Jesse, who was diagnosed with autism at three, and three mollycoddled cats Trigger, Lulu, and Hobbes in a cozy, cavernous townhouse ornamented with blue roses hurricane lamps, geode heart candles, and vintage ads for Victorian inventions.

David Milley
David Milley has written and published since the 1970s. His work has appeared in *Painted Bride Quarterly, Bay Windows, RFD, Friends Journal,* and *Feral.*

Sharon Mitchell
>Author declined a bio.

James Mulhern
>James Mulhern's writing has appeared in literary journals over two hundred and fifty times and has been recognized with many awards. In 2015, Mr. Mulhern was granted a fully paid writing fellowship to Oxford University. A story was longlisted for the Fish Short Story Prize that same year. In 2017, he was nominated for a Pushcart Prize. Two of his novels were Finalists for the United Kingdom's Wishing Shelf Book Awards. His novel, *Give Them Unquiet Dreams*, was a *Kirkus Reviews Best Book of the Year*. He was shortlisted for the Aesthetica Creative Writing Award 2021 for his poetry.

James B. Nicola
>James B. Nicola's seven full-length poetry collections include *Fires of Heaven* and *Turns & Twists* (2021-2022). A returning contributor to *The Writer's Workout*, he has received a Dana Literary Award, two *Willow Review* awards, one Best of Net, one Rhysling, and ten Pushcart nominations. His nonfiction book *Playing the Audience* won a *Choice* award.

Trish Tyler
>Trish Tyler is a cancer survivor and a comedian in no particular order. She's finishing up her graduate degree in writing and everything she does is dedicated to her son– Henry.

Jennifer Weigel

Jennifer Weigel is a multi-disciplinary mixed media conceptual artist. Weigel utilizes a wide range of media to convey her ideas, including assemblage, drawing, fibers, installation, jewelry, painting, performance, photography, sculpture, video and writing. Much of her work touches on themes of beauty, identity (especially gender identity), memory & forgetting, and institutional critique. You can read more of her writing on her website here:
jenniferweigelwords.wordpress.com

Charlotte Young

Charlotte Young is currently pursuing a bachelor's degree in English at the University of Idaho. She aspires to teach English at the college level so that she can share the beauty of words with others. Her writing is inspired by the world and people around her. She started writing poetry in her junior year of high school, and hopes to keep on creating throughout her life.

About the Editor

Theresa Green

Theresa is a co-founder of The Writer's Workout, a developmental editor, and a crime fiction writer.
www.premierliterary.com

A very special thank you to
Jessica Morris-Reade and Leigh Davis.

The Writer's Workout is a registered 501(c)(3) nonprofit organization.

Mission:
The Writer's Workout strives to provide a motivating atmosphere that fosters self-growth and development through encouraging language and education.
We want to help you be a better writer.

WW appreciates your support.

www.writersworkout.net

Printed in Great Britain
by Amazon